ATLANTIC OCEAN

CONNEMARA

Topographical Profile of Conor's Journey

www.randomhouse.com/kids

Library of Congress Cataloging-in-Publication Data
Ó Flatharta, Antoine. The prairie train / written by Antoine Ó Flatharta ;
illustrated by Eric Rohmann. p. cm.
Summary: As a young Irish immigrant boy travels by steam
engine across the American prairie to a new life, memories
of the old country pull at his heart.
[1. Immigrants–Fiction. 2. Locomotives–Fiction. 3. Railroads–Trains–
Fiction.] I. Rohmann, Eric, ill. II. Title.
PZ7.O331275Pr
1999
[Fic]–dc21   97-22021

ISBN 0-517-70988-0 (trade)
ISBN 0-517-70989-9 (lib. bdg.)

Printed in Hong Kong
10 9 8 7 6 5 4 3 2 1
First Edition

For Eoin

–A. O.

THE PRAIRIE TRAIN

by Antoine Ó Flatharta

illustrated by Eric Rohmann

Crown Publishers, Inc. ♛ New York

Once upon a time,
there was a train
that dreamed
of being
a boat.
This was a time when trains
were new and wonderful things.
A time when trains blew clouds
of steam. A time when train
engines were as shiny and as
extraordinary as rocket ships.

The train that dreamed of being a boat traveled through a vast, flat prairie in a land called the New World. Though in fact this world was very old and people had lived there long before the shiny new train tracks were nailed into the ground. Now the tracks stretched from sea to sea across the entire New World.

It seemed to the Prairie Train that the tracks went on forever. On and on in one long, flat straight line. The Prairie Train longed to be an old-fashioned boat with billowing sails, to take a journey that wasn't set by tracks.

One day, a boy named Conor arrived in the city of Chicago with his mother and father. They had come from a place called Connemara. A place on the edge of a faraway island. They had sailed across the Atlantic Ocean to land in New York, on the shores of America. Now they were about to start the final part of their journey on the Prairie Train.

Before Conor left Connemara, his grandfather, who was a boatbuilder, carved him a toy boat so that Conor would always remember him and the old world he was leaving behind.

Conor held the toy boat tightly in his hand and looked in wonder at the big train engine.

The train station was alive with people, all patiently waiting to board the Prairie Train. They came from faraway places with names like Krakow, Hull, Zagreb, Verona, Inverness, Kronoberg, and Connemara. The Prairie Train was waiting to carry them to new places. Places with names like Omaha, Kansas, Cheyenne, San Francisco.

As the train left Chicago behind and headed toward the big, flat prairies, Conor stared at his small wooden boat and thought about his grandfather.

The voices of the grownups filled the train with sounds that Conor had never heard before. They talked in the languages of the Old World. Conor listened to the voices as the Prairie Train traveled through towering grass that moved in the wind like gigantic green waves.

The train came to a curve, and
Conor put his head out the
window to better see the engine.
It looked so shiny and new. It
looked so strong. It looked as if
it could travel all the way around
the world without stopping. Conor
waved at the engine.

Then, as Conor was waving, his grandfather's boat fell out of the window and disappeared into the towering, billowing grass.

"Stop," cried Conor. "My boat! My boat is gone!"

"We can't stop the train, Conor," said his mother.

"I'll make you another boat," said his father.

"It wouldn't be the same," said Conor. "Please stop the train."

His mother gently told him once again, "We can't stop the train." And other people in the carriage said in their different languages, "Can't stop the train, Conor. Can't stop the train." Soon even the sound of the train itself seemed to say it: "Can't stop the train. Can't stop the train. Can't stop the train."

"I want to go home," Conor sobbed.
The other passengers looked at
Conor sadly. They knew how he felt.
They tried to comfort him. But all
Conor could think of was his wooden
boat, now lost forever somewhere out
on the great prairie.

The Prairie Train wanted so much to
comfort this sad little boy so far from
home. It started to bounce and shake
gently from side to side. Its wheels
started to make a shushing sound:
shussha, shussha, shussha, shussha . . .

It was now late evening, and Conor's father told Conor to try to get some sleep. "When you wake up, we'll be nearer our new home," he told Conor.

The Prairie Train continued to sing its lullaby: *shussha, shussha, shussha, shussha* . . .

Soon Conor began to fall asleep. And he started to dream. He dreamed about his grandfather making boats by the sea in Connemara. Big boats, small boats, long and narrow boats. And toy boats.

And then a strange thing happened.

The Prairie Train entered Conor's
dream. It wasn't on the prairie anymore.
It wasn't traveling on straight lines of tracks.
It was out in the middle of the ocean.
Free to move in any direction.
   Conor couldn't believe his eyes when he
looked out the window. They were sailing
on the sea! It was a moonlit night, and the
train was riding on top of silvery waves.
It was the greatest feeling in the world to
be in this train out in the middle of the sea.
It was better than any boat that Conor had
ever seen or been in.

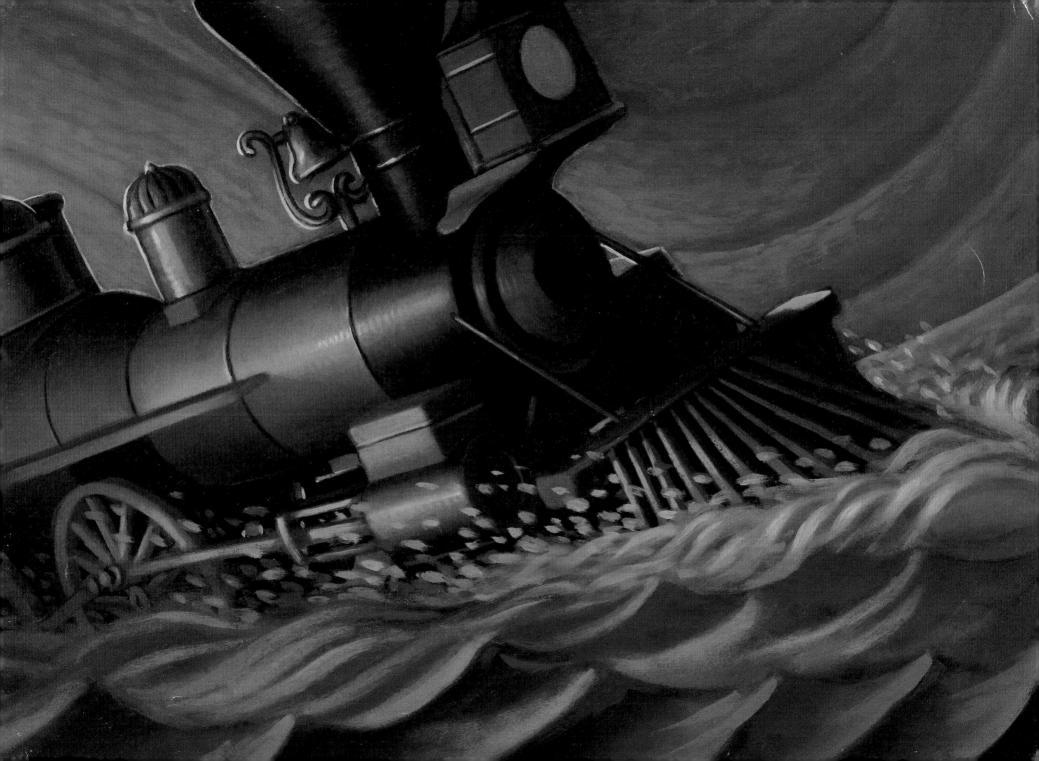

The Prairie Train moved faster and faster along the waves. Cut loose from its prairie tracks, it rocked and swayed along the wave tops.

"So this is what it's like to be a boat," it said.

It sailed on and on toward a distant craggy shoreline.

Conor looked out at the waves. He looked
up at the moon. It was so full and round it
seemed near enough to touch. Conor could
see the shore now and on it a man waving
to him.

The train rolled up and down with the
waves, getting closer and closer to the shore.
Soon Conor was close enough to see that
the man was his grandfather.

"Hello, Conor!" shouted the old man.

"I lost the boat you made me," said Conor.

"What harm," shouted the old man.

"But I miss it and now I'm sad," said Conor.

"There's bigger boats waiting for you,"
said the old man.

"Where?" asked Conor.

"In the city you're sailing to," said the old
man. "It has boats and ships, carriages and
trains. It's a beautiful city built on a bay.
It's all there waiting for you, Conor."

The train slowed down until it was almost at a standstill. The Prairie Train wanted to enjoy every second of this sea-sailing night.

"See that moon?" said Conor's grandfather. "It's the same moon that's shining on all of us. Makes no difference if you're in Connemara or San Francisco. It's the same moon we're all looking up at."

As Conor continued to stare at the moon, his sadness started to melt away. And all of a sudden he began to feel a great urge to see this new city they were sailing to.

The Prairie Train felt this need as well now. It turned and headed out to sea.

As they turned, the moon began to fade and the sun began to rise. Right before his eyes, Conor could see the waves turning into a swaying sea of grass. They were back on the prairie.

Early morning sunlight started to flood the carriage, waking the passengers. Everyone was glad to see Conor feeling better.

"All he needed was a good rest," said Conor's mother.

Conor looked out the window. He could see
the engine up ahead, pulling the train steadily
westward.

As the morning sun climbed higher and
higher in the sky, Conor and the Prairie Train
moved forward together.

Issued by CHICAGO, R. ISLAND & PACIFIC R. R.
SPECIAL EMIGRANT TICKET.
Chicago to SAN FRANCISCO
GOOD FOR
One EMIGRANT Passage.
(IN EMIGRANT CARS ONLY.)
Only on presentation of this Ticket, with Checks
attached, and good only for 20 days from date.
CONDITIONS—In consideration of this ticket being sold by the
C. R. I. & P. R. R. at a reduced price from the regular first class rate
it is hereby understood and agreed upon by the purchaser, that it
will be good for passage if presented within twenty (20) days (only)
from _____ 187_ after which
time it will be void
104
General Ticket Agent.

Issued by CHICAGO, ROCK ISLAND & PACIFIC RAILROAD
CENTRAL PACIFIC R. R.
Good in Emigrant Cars Only.
UNION JUNCTION
TO
SAN FRANCISCO.
No Stop-Over Check will be given on this Ticket.
E 031 | This Check not good if detached. | EMIGRA
104

San Francisco

Cheyenne

Omaha

Chicago

New York